"Mac" the Macaw

A true story by
Gerard R. Wolfe

With illustrations by
Neil David, Sr.
Hopi Artist

ISBN 1-4196-3708-8

To order additional copies, please contact us.
BookSurge, LLC
www.booksurge.com
1-866-308-6235
orders@booksurge.com

"Mac" the Macaw

Part 1

"Hello Mac!"

Contents

page

Mac in the jungle

Part 1

"Hello Mac!"

1. Mac Leaves the Jungle

Deep in the jungle of South America, Mac the Macaw lived in the tall treetops with his brothers and sisters. He was a large macaw--a big bird that looked like a giant parrot. Mac had a beautiful red body, green wings, and very long blue tail feathers. He had a huge white beak that was strong enough to crack the tasty Brazil nuts that he liked so much. He and his brothers and sisters loved to eat sunflower seeds, and lots of fruit like bananas, oranges, mangos, and grapes.

Macaws love to fly over tall trees and scream "Caw! Caw! Caw!" They can be heard from far away, as they glide above the branches looking for another comfortable perch and more fruit to eat. Sometimes they meet other macaws of different colors and they yell and squawk back and forth to see who can scream the loudest. They make so much noise, that other birds often fly away, and the animals run off into the forest.

Mac enjoyed flying in the jungle with his friends and family, but one day a man climbed up the tree where Mac was perched and lured him with several pieces of fruit. When Mac was close enough, the man threw a net over him and slowly climbed down the tree with him. "Squawk! Squawk! Squawk!" screamed Mac, but he was trapped and could not fly away. When the man reached the ground, he put the bird into a large cage. He then put the cage on a small truck and drove away.

After a while they arrived at an open field where an airplane was waiting. The driver quickly put the cage with Mac in it into the plane. He spoke with the pilot and another man who was standing there, and in a few minutes the plane took off.

The plane flew for many hours, and when it finally landed, Mac looked out the open door, but could not see any jungle. At the airport there were no trees, only buildings that were higher than the trees that he used to live in. He could see no birds, no animals, no fruit—only many planes. He also heard strange, loud noises from the planes, trucks, and cars, and also from people who were milling around on the ground.

Then someone loaded him in his cage onto a big truck, and they drove off to the city.

2. Mac is Adopted by an Opera Singer

The truck delivered Mac to a pet shop in the city where he was placed in a smaller cage next to other birds and many animals he had never seen before. When they saw Mac they began crowing, chirping, barking, and meowing, all at once. Mac had never heard such sounds before and he became frightened. After a while, however, he discovered that the animals were really just saying hello to him, and he began squawking back to them. He discovered many different animals that he had never seen before--cats, dogs, hamsters, rabbits, and lots of new kinds of colorful birds.

A few days later, a lady who was once a famous opera singer, came into the pet shop and asked the shopkeeper "Do you have any big birds for sale who can speak?" "Yes, ma'am, " he said, "we just received a huge red macaw from South America, but he doesn't talk, he only screams."

When the lady saw Mac, she exclaimed "What a lovely bird! What a beautiful macaw! I know that macaws are very smart, and like parrots, they can easily learn to talk. He will learn to talk very well and I will even teach him how to sing!"

Just then Mac cried out, "M-a-a-a-c!" And the lady said, "My goodness, he just told me his name. It sounded just like 'Mac!'" "And, Mac is a very good name for a mac-aw, isn't it?

The lady paid the pet shop owner who placed Mac in a brand-new cage, and she took Mac home in a taxi. She then moved Mac to a room with several other animals. He became very excited, as all around the room there were parrots, parakeets, canaries, pigeons, two dogs, and a pussycat. But he was the only macaw, and he felt a little lonely.

3. Mac Learns How to Talk

When Mac became used to his new surroundings, the lady thought that now she would begin to teach Mac how to talk. She came to his cage and said, "Now listen to me, Mac, I was a famous opera singer, and I was also a school teacher, and you are going to learn to talk!" She then held up an apple close to the cage and said loudly, "Apple! Apple!" Mac would have loved to eat that delicious apple, but the lady didn't give it to him, but just kept saying "APPLE, APPLE, APPLE!" She wanted to teach Mac to say "apple," and then she would give it to him. That way Mac would learn to ask for an apple by saying "apple."

Mac tried very hard, but all that came out was "A-a-a----CAW!"
"That's not bad for the first time," said the lady. "Let's try again." She came very close to Mac's cage, and in a very friendly voice repeated, "A-p-p-l-e, a-a-a-p-p-l-e." Then she cut off a small piece and handed it to him. Mac grabbed it with one of his claws and put it into his beak. He thought it really tasted good!

"That's even better, Mac, you will learn very quickly," and she gave him the rest of the apple as a reward for trying so hard.

Mac seemed very pleased with himself, and after finishing the apple, he kept saying over and over, "a-a-p, a-a-p, a-a-p." He opened his big beak as wide as he could, and . . .out came "A-P-P-L-E!"

In the meantime, the lady had gone out of the room and did not hear Mac. When she returned, she heard Mac repeat, "A-P-P-L-E, a-p-p-l-e, A-P-P-L-E!"

"one ... two ... three ..."

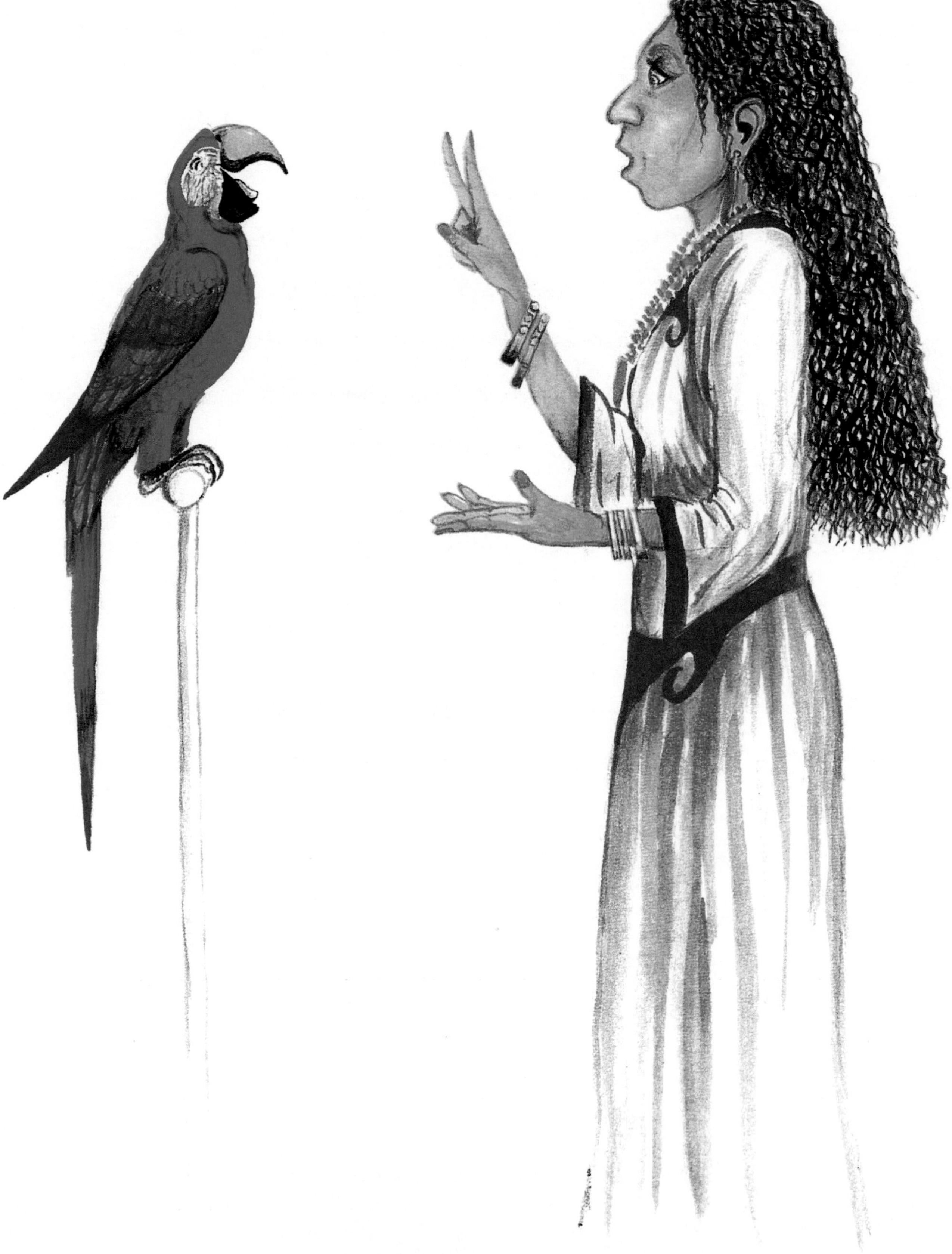

"How wonderful!" she exclaimed, "You said it perfectly!" and she gave him another piece of apple. Mac seemed very happy, and for the rest of the day, all he said was "A-P-P-L-E, a-p-p-l-e, A-P-P-L-E," over and over again, and each time the lady handed him still another chunk of apple. Later in the evening, when he finished his regular dinner of sunflower seeds, the lady said, "Now here is your last piece of apple for today. You have eaten up all my apples.""

The next morning, the lady said, "Today I will teach you another word." In her hand she held a nice, ripe banana, one of Mac's favorite fruits. Again very slowly she said, "Banana, b-a-n-a-n-a, b-a-a-n-a-a-n-a-a. "Now you try it, Mac!"

Mac loved bananas and really wanted that one. So he tried, and out came, "B-a-a, b-a-a-n-A-P-P-L-E " "Oh, no, no, no," laughed the lady. "You got all mixed up. Now listen again," and she said, "b-a-n-a-n-a" several times.

Mac cocked his head to one side and listened very carefully. "b-a-n-a-n-a, B-A-N-A-N-A! BANANA!" He did it! "B-A-N-A-N-A, b-a-n-a-n-a, B-A-N-A-N-A!" he screamed. The lady was so happy that she began jumping up and down. "What a clever bird you are!" Mac also started bouncing up and down on his perch. "Why, Mac, you copycat! You're jumping up and down, just as I did." Mac then got the banana, which he carefully held in his claw as he slowly peeled it with his beak.

In a few weeks Mac learned to say "orange" and "strawberry," and many other words, and such funny things as "Hello," "Good boy!" "Give me a kiss!" and even "Up and Down, Up and Down!" while he bounced on his perch.

One day the lady said to him, "Mac, now it's time to learn how to count." She repeated over and over. . . "one. . .two. . .three. . ." And when Mac learned to say them, she went on, "four. . .five. . .six. . .! Pick up Sticks!"

In a short time Mac could be heard counting out loud, "one. . .two. . .three. . .four. . five. . six. . . Pick up Sticks!" Sometimes he would forget one of the numbers, and the lady would say, "Mac, you made a mistake, go back and try again, you skipped a number!" He did try again, and always got it right the second or third time. The lady was very surprised when Mac would sometimes skip a number, and then by himself, he began counting all over again.

The lady had two tiny dogs named Henrietta and Bridgit. They liked to bark a lot. Whenever they barked too loudly--which was very often--she said to them very strictly, "Henrietta . Bridgit. . .Be quiet!" Mac watched them very carefully, and soon. . .guess what! He began to imitate their barking by screaming "Woof. . .Woof!" And then, to the lady's amazement, he then said, "Henrietta . . . Bridgit. . . Be quiet!" So not only did the lady tell the little dogs to stop barking, but Mac also told them.

Mac liked to watch the pussycat that often curled up next to his cage. You can imagine how funny it must have sounded when after a while Mac began to say "Meow, Meow." Sometimes when Mac cried "meow" very loudly, the lady came running into the room thinking that it was really her cat calling her. Then she looked at Mac and laughed. "You fooled me, you funny bird!"

In a few weeks, Mac was imitating the sounds of all the other animals.

4. Mac Gets Singing Lessons

"Mac, you are learning to talk very well," said the lady. "Now you are going to learn how to sing. Not long ago I was a famous opera singer, and I still love to sing. You never heard me, because I always practice in the other room. Now I am going to sing for you here, and maybe you will learn to sing, too."

The lady began to sing: ah,ah,ah,ah,ah,ah,ah, several times very loudly.

Mac just listened quietly. Then she sang even louder, ah,ah,ah,ah,ah,ah,ah,ah.

"ah ah ah ah ah ah ah"

But Mac still said nothing."

Oh well," she said, "we'll try again tomorrow."

The next day she tried again, but Mac just sat still. Finally he opened up his beak wide and screamed "**CAW! CAW! CAW!**"

"Oh, Mac, that's not very good," said the lady. "I think you will just have to pay more attention," and again her voice rose up with: ah,ah,ah,ah,ah,ah,ah,ah,ah!

This time Mac looked much more interested. He cocked his head and seemed to listen very closely. Again the lady practiced her singing, but much, much louder. Suddenly Mac began bouncing up and down. The lady sang and sang, and Mac kept bouncing up and down. But he still didn't say a word.

"Well, Mac, I think you really like my voice. After a few days maybe, you will try to sing." And for the next week the lady sang and sang. But Mac just listened quietly.

After breakfast one morning, as the lady was washing the dishes, she began to sing, ah,ah,ah,ah,ah,ah,ah,ah! . .and to her amazement, from the cage across the room came: ah,ah,ah,ah,ah,ah,ah,ah,ah,ah,ah! It was Mac! "My goodness!" exclaimed the lady, "You ARE singing! Oh, how happy I am! That sounds just like me, practicing!"

Mac continued singing as loudly as he could, bouncing up and down while he sang. He seemed to enjoy singing so much that he sang all day long, only stopping to eat and drink. And the lady was so happy that she clapped her hands with joy.

From then on, whenever the lady sang, Mac would join in. "Aren't we having a wonderful time!" said the lady. "You will surely end up singing in the Metropolitan Opera," she laughed.

5. Mac Has Fun with Accidents in the Kitchen

One day the lady accidentally dropped a big plate that fell to the floor with a loud crash and broke into many pieces. "Oh, what have I done?" she cried, "for it was my biggest and nicest plate." Mac, who saw the accident, started rocking up and down, and screamed "Oh, what have I done! Oh, what have I done!" exactly the way the lady said it. At first she was shocked, but then, even though she had broken her best plate, she burst out laughing, and kept laughing so hard, that she accidentally dropped a teacup. And when Mac heard the crash of the cup on the floor, he cried out "Oh, what have I done! Oh, what have I done!"

Mac and the lady had become very good friends. She really loved that bird, and Mac was very fond of her, too. But one thing used to annoy the lady. Every once in a while Mac would let out a very loud shriek, that would scare her and the other animals. She didn't like such sudden loud noises.

She then stared at Mac and shouted at him in as loud a voice as she could, "Stop that screaming! WILL YOU STOP THAT SCREAMING!"

Mac, who by now had become a very good listener, would repeat what he was taught. So what happened was, Mac would scream "CAW, C-A-W," but then follow it by yelling "Stop that screaming! WILL YOU STOP THAT SCREAMING!"

6. The Old Lady Gets Sick

After almost a year, Mac learned so many new words that the lady couldn't remember all the things he could say. She was now getting quite old and could no longer work or take care of all her nice pets. She called a neighbor friend to ask what she should do. "I'm afraid I'll have to give away all these wonderful friends--Henrietta, Bridgit, the parakeets, the parrot, the pigeon, the canaries, the hamsters, the pussycat . . . and Mac! She was very, very sad because she did not want to part with them, especially not with Mac, who had become her favorite.

Her neighbor said she could only take care of the pussycat, and that was all. So the lady called the Humane Society, and they said they would come and take the animals and try to find new homes for them. But she could not bear to give up Mac. Her neighbor told her that she had just spoken to a young professor from the nearby university, and that he would be very happy to take care of Mac because he liked parrots and parakeets, and recently one of his parakeets had died. Of course he realized that Mac was much, much bigger than a parakeet or parrot.

A few days later the other animals were taken to the Humane Society, and the old lady learned that many nice people had adopted them. She felt good that they would be well taken care of and that they would be happy in their new homes. She hoped that Mac, too, would like his new home.

Soon she had to go to a nursing home, but she never forgot her animal friends, especially her best pupil, Mac. At first she was very sad and lonely in the nursing home, but when she would think about Mac and how funny he was, and all the things he used to say, she began to smile, and then she laughed. She began telling the nurses who were taking care of her all about Mac.

"Mac was a very good pupil," said the lady. "He learned how to count up to six; he could name lots of fruits, like apple, banana, strawberry, and orange. He could even call my dogs by name, imitate their barking by saying 'woof, woof,' and then tell them to be quiet." The nurses were really amused and asked the lady to tell them more about Mac, and also tell the other people in the nursing home, which would surely would practice singing, because she had been a famous opera singer, and how Mac began imitating her voice, and pretty soon he, too, was singing. The people in the nursing home were always delighted to hear all those stories.

Mac escapes from his cage

7. Mac is Adopted by a Professor and Taken to College

The professor who adopted Mac was very happy to have him as a pet. Every day Mac surprised him with all the words he knew. He bought Mac a larger cage and decided to move him to his office at the university. He did not want to leave Mac alone all day in his apartment, and besides, he loved to listen to Mac talking. Everyone in the office liked Mac, and they, too, began to teach him all kinds of new things to say.

One of the secretaries in the office, whose name was Fran, thought it would be nice to teach Mac to say things that would make people laugh. So when everyone went home at the end of the day, she stayed with Mac, and taught him to say such funny things as "Hello, Mac!" "Wanna cracker?" and "HELP, H-E-L-P ME!" He loved to yell "Help" so loudly and clearly, that when strangers came into the office, they thought he was really screaming for help. Once, when he was yelling "HELP ME!" several people who were working in nearby offices heard the screams and came running, thinking someone was really in serious trouble. At first they couldn't believe that it was a bird, because his voice was so loud and clear.

8. Mac Escapes from His Cage

Mac loved getting all this attention, and hated being kept in a cage with bars. So the professor and a friend of his built him a huge glass cage, so that he could see everything around him. The cage had a large door with a hook on the front, so that it would be easy to open and give him food and water. But Mac still did not like being closed up in a cage, and he began watching when someone opened the door to see how the hook worked. Then one day when the professor came to work, he was astonished to see that Mac had escaped from his cage, climbed down, and walked across the floor to the professor's office and climbed up on his chair. There he was, sitting on the arm of the chair, and as the professor approached, Mac greeted him, saying "Hel-lo, gimme a kiss!"

"How on earth did you get out, Mac?" asked the professor. "Did someone let him out?" he wondered. That night he asked the man who cleaned the office if he had opened Mac's cage, but the man said no. The man, whose name was Bill, liked Mac very much, and every night they would talk to each other, but he said that Mac was always locked in his cage.

That night, before the professor went home, he made sure that the hook on Mac's cage was closed. But next morning Mac was out again! Everyone in the office was very curious to find out how he got out. Well, they soon found out, because that afternoon while they were busy working, Fran, one of the office secretariies, cried out, "Look everybody, Mac has figured out how to open his cage!" And indeed, Mac, with his sharp-pointed beak poked through the crack in the door and lifted the hook, and the door swung open. . .and out he came, climbing up to the roof of his cage. Everyone marveled at how clever a bird he was!

9. Mac Learns to Fly Again

Since Mac liked to be out of his cage so much, the professor decided to let Mac climb on top of his cage whenever he wanted. He seemed to enjoy sitting high up, watching everything that went on in the office. Mac had been living in a cage for a long time, and had forgotten how to fly. The professor also built him a large perch outside the cage, with a seed cup attached to one end, and a water cup to the other. And there Mac sat all day long, but at night he was put back into the cage. . .this time with a much better lock on it. He seemed quite content in the university office, but the professor wondered whether he was really happy. After all, thought the professor, birds love to fly, but Mac has forgotten. "Can we teach him to fly again?" "Can people really teach birds how to fly?" "And what would happen in the office if he started flying again?" The professor then asked some of the other instructors who often came to the office, "Can a person teach a bird to fly?" Nobody seemed to know.

"Well, I'm going to try," said the professor, and he went to get Mac. The bird always liked to climb on a large stick if the professor held one in front of him. That was how he carried Mac around. It wasn't a good idea to carry Mac on his arm, because Mac's claws were so sharp. And besides, Mac loved to chew on things, so it wouldn't be safe to have him sitting on his arm if Mac suddenly decided to do some chewing with his sharp beak. The professor remembered how Mac could easily snap a pencil in half if he felt like.

The professor then began the experiment. He took the thick stick, and Mac climbed on. He began running around the office with Mac, and as he ran, and the breeze blew across Mac's feathers, Mac lifted his wings as if he were about to take off. But he just sat there, enjoying the free ride.

Again and again, the professor ran back and forth across the office with Mac clinging to the stick. But the bird wouldn't fly. Maybe he figured that it was easier to be carried than to fly. Everyone laughed very hard to see the professor dashing around in the office with a big bird on a long stick. "Whoever heard of teaching a bird to fly?"

Someone said that maybe the professor should stick to teaching his students and not fooling around with a bird. "But I think I can teach him," replied the professor. "After all, he did learn how to speak, and I've taught him many new things, and by golly, he'll learn to fly again!" So he kept on running around the office with Mac perched on the stick.

Then the professor had an idea. "If I very gently push him off the stick, perhaps he'll catch on and will try to fly." So he again ran with Mac, this time holding the stick closer to the floor. If Mac wouldn't fly, he would not hurt himself if he fell off. As the professor ran, he slowly began pushing the bird off the stick, and Mac then started to squawk loudly and flap his large wings. "Fly, Mac . . .fly!" shouted the professor, and he kept on shoving Mac off as he ran.

But the professor accidentally pushed him a little too hard, and . . . Plop! Mac lost his balance, and fell off the stick, landing on the floor and squawking loudly. The professor quickly

Mac gets a *flying lesson*

helped him up with the stick and tried again. Plop! Mac again lost his balance and fell down. "Caw! . . Caw! . . Caw!" screamed Mac, as he picked himself up and waddled clumsily on the floor.

"All right, Mac, that's enough for today, we'll try again tomorrow," said the professor, and he carried Mac back to his cage, where he continued to squawk loudly and then yelled "Stop that screaming!" The professor gave him an apple as a reward for trying to fly, and said he'd give him more of his favorite foods if he tried again next morning.

Two more days passed with Mac still tumbling off the stick, but the professor noticed that he was now flapping his wings much harder. "Maybe he'll catch on one of these days." On the third day, as the professor slowly pushed Mac off the stick, Mac began flapping his wings harder than ever, and . . . instead of falling to the floor, he took off into the air, made a quick turn around the office, and sank slowly to the floor!

"Attaboy, Mac!" shouted the professor. "I think you've got it! You flew . . .you really flew!" Everyone in the office clapped and cheered, and Mac squawked louder than before! "Do you want to try it again, Mac?" asked the professor, as he picked him up with the stick. Mac seemed to understand, and stepped quickly onto the stick. This time when the professor ran with him, Mac didn't wait to be pushed off, but he leaped into the air with his wings flapping wildly, and flew round and round the office for several minutes. And when the professor called to him and held out the stick, Mac landed beautifully on it, saying "Hel-lo!"

"I'm so proud of you, Mac," said the professor, "you really learned how to fly again!" and he gave him a big slice of orange and a few peanuts. And he called out to everyone in the nearby offices to come see Mac fly.

10. Mac Gets Mischievous

Now that Mac had learned how to fly again, everyone in the office had to be careful. He would suddenly take off from his perch and circle the room, landing on things other than where he belonged, including the secretaries' desks. There was a fireplace at one end of the office, and Mac liked to land on the mantelpiece above it, running back and forth saying his favorite words. If there was anything on the mantelpiece, it soon landed with a crash below, as Mac always enjoyed picking things up and dropping them to the floor.

When Mac would occasionally land on the desks of the secretaries, Fran and Phyllis, and would watch them as they worked. They enjoyed having Mac stare at them, but once in a while he would steal pencils and fly back to his cage with them. He loved those pencils, because he could scratch his back and neck with them. He would then snap them in two with his powerful beak and chew them into little splinters. That, of course, did not please the secretaries very much.

One of Mac's favorite things to eat was ice cream. Whenever anyone in the office was about to finish an ice cream bar, they would give him the stick, and he would hold it in his claw while he licked the rest of the ice cream off with his thick round tongue. Then he would keep the stick and scratched himself with it. Sometimes he would let the professor scratch his neck with the stick, or even with his fingers, but that could be a bit dangerous, because of Mac's very big and sharp beak.

Macaws all love to chew on things. That helps keep their beaks sharp, but with Mac, that caused some problems. Mac used to chew on his seed cup, but it was made of metal and he couldn't do much damage to it. One day he reached under the cup, and with his beak he clamped onto the screw nut that fastened the cup to the perch. He began to twist it, and the cup slowly loosened. In no time the cup became unscrewed and fell off, spilling seeds on the floor of his cage. He must have thought that was great fun, because he then began twisting off the

Mac unscrews his seed cup

water cup at the other end of the perch. Splash! The cup and water went down, too. Mac then squawked loudly and flapped his wings, as if to say "Look what a great job I've done!"

Fran, who liked Mac a lot, was afraid he would get hungry and thirsty, so she picked up the cups and re-attached them to the perch. She then got him a fresh supply of sunflower seeds and water, and went back to her desk.

No sooner did she turn her back when Mac was at it again, unscrewing his two cups and dumping his seeds and water all over the floor of the cage!

"You're a naughty bird!" she cried. "Now you'll be without food and water. See how you like that!" She went back to the cage, cleaned up the mess, and after a few minutes said, "O.K., I'll give you one last chance, Mac." And again she screwed the cups on his perch and filled them with seeds and water, and she stayed there watching him.

But Mac paid no attention. He again leaned over and unscrewed his cups, and. . .Splash! Crash! First the water cup, then the seed cup. Some of the water and seeds even splashed on Fran's dress and shoes. "Now you'll have to be punished," screamed Fran, as she ran to the professor's office to tell him what happened.

"Professor, I can't handle that mean old bird," said Fran. "Will you please come here and fix what Mac has done?" And she ran out to get some rags to help clean her dress and shoes and wipe up the mess at the bottom of Mac's cage. The professor got a large screwdriver and put the cups back on, tightening the screws with all his might. Now Mac's strong beak could no longer unscrew them.

Mac watched quietly and when the professor finished and went back to his office, the bird once more turned to his cups and tried to remove them. But this time he couldn't. They were on too tight, and Mac began to squawk louder than ever, "CAW! CAW! CAW!

"Stop that screaming!"

The secretaries became very annoyed and yelled at him, "Mac, stop that screaming! "Will you stop that screaming!" And what did Mac do? He just squawked even louder, and then shouted back at them, **"STOP THAT SCREAMING! WILL YOU STOP THAT SCREAMING!"** He had never said that before, and the professor and the secretaries couldn't help laughing. Even Fran, who was still a little angry with Mac, couldn't help saying that it was a very funny thing to come from Mac, and that he was really a very clever bird.

Mac then repeated "Stop that screaming!" several times, and everyone in the office just laughed. Mac then quieted down and it seemed that he was trying to imitate the people laughing, but all that came out was "caw-ca-caw-ca-caw," although Fran said that it did sound a little like laughter, and she went to his cage and gave him a peanut.

"Mac" the Macaw

Part 2

Mac is Back!

Contents

"Mac" the Macaw

Part 2

Mac is Back

1. Mac is Very Naughty

Not everybody liked having Mac around. Fran and Mary, two of the three office secretaries, were very fond of Mac, so was Zeki, one of the young office clerks. But Phyllis, the third secretary, did not like him and wished he would go away. Mac must have known she didn't like him, for every once in a while he would fly over her desk, opening his beak and dropping seed shells on her. "Mac, I'll fix you one of these days!" she growled, as she shook her fist at him, and swept away the empty shells into a wastebasket.

Mac always had a big appetite and would eat almost anything. Not only did he eat nearly a pound of sunflower seeds every day, he also ate all kinds of fruit and nuts. But no matter how much he ate, he always seemed hungry for more. That was one of the reasons that Phyllis didn't like him, as you will see.

One day she was eating lunch at her desk and was about to take another bite of a big juicy hamburger, when she was called away from the room for a moment. Mac had been watching her closely. As soon as Phyllis left, he swooped down from the top of his cage, landed on her desk, grabbed the rest of her hamburger in his big beak, and quickly flew back to his cage with it.

When Phyllis returned, she was astonished to find her plate empty, and asked angrily, "Who took my hamburger?" Everyone had been very busy working and nobody had seen Mac fly down and grab it. Then she looked up and saw Mac holding her hamburger in his claw, calmly digging out large chunks of it with his beak. Everyone roared with laughter, and said,

Enjoying his stolen hamburger

"Who ever heard of a bird eating a hamburger?" But Phyllis didn't think it was funny at all, and went to the professor's office to complain. "I can't stand that bird," she cried, "He stole my lunch and flew away with it!"

The professor smiled. "I don't expect that Mac will pay you for the hamburger," he said, "so I will go out and buy you another." He then told everyone in the office, "From now on, please do not leave any food around for Mac to steal. As you have seen, that bird will eat anything!"

Fran and Mary, however, still kept sneaking food to Mac. And as he ate, they would ask him if that was good. A few days later when Mac was watching people eating, they heard him ask, "Is that good?" Everyone (except Phyllis) thought that was really so comical. Another time, when he asked Mac if he liked what he was eating, to his astonishment Mac replied, "M-m-m, that's good!" Everyone wondered how Mac had learned to say that, just at the right moment. From then on, whenever he really liked something that he was eating, and someone asked him if he liked it, he always replied, "M-m-m. that's good!"

2. Mac Causes More Trouble

Mac liked to fly in and out of the professor's office when the door was open. He would swoop down on the desk, landing on the arm of the desk lamp. Mac was much too heavy for it, and the lamp would collapse and dump him onto whatever was lying on the desk. Papers, pencils, and books would go flying in every direction! The professor was not at all pleased with that. Once Mac landed very hard, and not only sent everything flying, but also knocked over a cup of coffee that soaked everything on the desk, making a dreadful mess.

"This has got to stop, Mac," shouted the professor angrily, "or I will put you back in your cage for good." Mac seemed to understand, and did not come back to the desk anymore, but he did manage to find many other naughty things to do.

AH - AH - AH

Playing peek-a-boo

Macaws must keep their beaks sharp to be able to crack nuts and seeds, and the professor always gave him lots of things to chew on. One morning when the professor opened the office, he discovered that Mac had flown up to the line of telephone wires that were strung along the wall near the ceiling, and was chewing on them. Many of the wires were twisted and hanging loose. And would you believe! Mac had succeeded in knocking out all the telephone lines in the building and all the phones were now dead.

"Mac, what have you done this time?" cried everyone when they saw the loose wires. When the telephone company repairman came, he was very angry with Mac and spoke very loudly to him, saying, "Birds don't belong in offices, especially birds that eat telephone wires!" He told the professor that Mac should be kept in his cage where he could not do any more damage. But the professor thought he would give Mac just one more chance because everyone enjoyed having him fly free, and he hoped that the bird had learned his lesson and would behave better from now on.

From then on, Mac did not rip down any more telephone wires. Instead, he discovered that it was lots of fun to fly over to one of the wall cabinets, pull open the doors with his beak, and climb inside. Then he would reach out and close the doors behind him. As soon as the doors were shut, he sang as loudly as he could, ah,ah.ah,ah,ah,ah,ah,ah,ah, over and over again, just as the opera singer had taught him. The sound of his voice from inside the cabinet imitating hers always amused everyone, and all work in the office would come to a halt as they listened.

Mac would then quietly open one door, slowly stick his head out and look around to see if anyone was watching, then would say in a friendly tone, "Coo-Coo! Coo-Coo!" and quickly pull the door closed again. He repeated this peek-a-boo act many times and must have thought it a great trick.

Mac greets the friendly mice.

3. Mac Gets Visits from Friendly Mice

Mac ate mostly in his cage, and many small pieces of food sometimes dropped to the bottom. The professor did clean his cage every day, but there were always a few nutshells and fruit peels lying below. One morning as the professor came into his office, he saw Mac leaning down from his perch toward the bottom of the cage, saying, "Hello, Hel-lo!" He wondered whom Mac could be talking to at the bottom of the cage. The professor drew closer, and to his surprise there were two little brown field mice running around among the nutshells and fruit peels. They didn't notice the professor, who kept very quiet as he watched them. The little mice seemed to be playing, chasing each other while looking for scraps of food. They kept running in circles while Mac looked down at them, saying "Hello, Hel-lo!" over and over again. Mac and the professor had fun watching the mice, but the secretaries, especially Phyllis, were not too happy about having mice in the office, even if they were just playful. "The mice are so cute," said the professor, "I don't have the heart to chase them. After all, they are Mac's friends, aren't they? "

4. Mac Meets Machka the Cat

Soon, Mac had another friend to keep him company. Peter, one of the young office clerks, had found a stray cat and brought it to the office. "I found him in the park. He didn't seem to belong to anyone, and was very hungry," he said, " so I took him home, but my parents wouldn't allow me to keep him. "Can we keep him in the office, professor? Please?" The cat was almost pure white and very friendly. The professor picked him up and said, "Well, let's first ask Mac."

Mac meets Matchka the cat

The professor held up the pussycat in his arms to introduce him to Mac. Mac leaned over, cocked his head, and called out very sweetly, "Hel-lo!" The professor then said, "Well. O.K., Peter, we'll let him stay for a couple of days and see how they get along together."

They seemed to get along fine, but the cat seemed a little frightened of Mac's big beak, and never got too close. At night after everyone went home, Bill, the cleaning man, felt that since Mac had a name, the cat should have one also, and he called him Machka. He explained, "In Jugoslavia, where I come from, that means 'pussycat' and every house always had a 'machka.'"

Mac and Machka were always friendly with each other, however the only place in the office where the two did not get along was on the mantelpiece, above the fireplace. Whenever the cat leaped up to sit there, Mac flew right over and tried to sit there too, but there was place only for one.

So they would quarrel--the pussycat meowing and swinging his paw at Mac, and Mac screaming back at him, trying to shove him off the mantelpiece with his beak. After a while neither one was able to make the other leave, so Mac gave up the struggle and flew back to his cage leaving the mantelpiece to Matchka.

By now you must know that Mac really loved getting attention. If nobody played with him for a while, he usually did something to get people to notice him or talk to him. First he would repeat many words, then count to six, and if that didn't work, he started screaming. He even yelled "Stop that screaming!" but he went on screaming anyway, until someone came close to his cage.

Mac takes a shower

5. Mac Takes a Shower

One day the professor saw Mac doing something unusual. He was dipping his big beak into his water cup and tossing drops of water over his back. He did it again and again. Could he be trying to take a bath, wondered the professor. So he brought a small pan of water and placed it near Mac's perch. The bird immediately stepped into it and began splashing water over himself with his beak.

"He really does want to bathe," said everyone. So the professor bought a small plant sprayer and filled it with water. He spread newspapers on the floor of the cage, and gently bathed Mac by squeezing water out of the sprayer.

Mac loved it! He spread his wings wide apart and raised his long tail so that the spray would cover him completely from head to tail. He turned around and around, and kept putting his head under the spray. When he had had enough, he shook his feathers to get the extra water off, but then came back for more. In a few minutes he became completely soaked, and the professor heard him saying, "M-m-m, m-m-m!"

After his bath, Mac climbed to the edge of the cage and attempted to fly across the room, but his feathers were too wet, and he came crashing down to the floor with a loud thud. The professor felt sorry for him, and he got a big towel, wrapped it around him, and carried him back to his cage. "No more flying while you're soaked, Mac," he said, and he closed the door to the cage. From then on, Mac got a shower bath twice a week. Every time Mac saw the professor coming with the sprayer, he immediately spread his wings and tail and began saying "M-m-m, m-m-m," as if to say "Give me another shower, I love to bathe." Everyone in the office always stopped work and enjoyed watching Mac take his shower.

Mac is warned by a policeman

6. Mac Almost Gets Arrested

Mac loved looking out of the window next to his cage. He had a second perch that stood nearby facing the street. Whenever he was alone in the office, he flew over to that perch and looked out. When people passed by, he banged on the glass with his beak to attract attention until someone heard the banging and came over. Once he banged so hard and kept yelling "H-e-l-p, H-E-L-P M-E!" so loudly that a group of people outside thought that he was really in trouble, and they called the police. Two policemen soon arrived. They opened the office door and went in to see who was screaming for help. When they came close to Mac, he greeted them with his usual "Hel-lo", and they realized that it was just a bird that had caused the commotion. When the people in the office heard about it, they had a big laugh, but the policemen didn't think it was funny. Before they left they told Mac that if he yelled "Help" when he didn't need any, they would come back and put him in a much bigger cage, called a jail!

7. Mac Likes Some People, but Not Others

Mac liked to have people around him, but he seemed to love the professor more than anyone else. He also liked girls who had long hair. Whenever a girl with long hair came into the office, he would squint his big red eyes, bounce up and down, and say over and over, "Gimme a kiss! Gimme a kiss!" and then he would make loud sucking noises with his tongue that sounded exactly like kisses.

There were also people whom he did not like. For some reason, he was not very fond of one of the teachers who came to the office almost every evening. The teacher did like Mac at first, but whenever she came close to his perch or his cage, Mac would raise his wings and hiss at her, and then he would let out a squawk and yell "GET OUT OF HERE! GET OUT OF HERE!" She was so startled that she ran out of the office and said, "That's no bird, he must be a devil!" Everyone was very curious where he had learned to say that, and wondered who had taught it to him, as nobody had ever heard him say it before. That was the last time the poor teacher came close to Mac.

8. Mac Gets Sick and Goes to the Hospital

One day Mac was sitting very still, and looked very droopy. He was as quiet as the mice who ran around in his cage. The professor looked at him very closely and guessed that he must be sick. He called the veterinarian at the animal hospital, who said, "Bring him right away, and we'll have a look at him."

The professor called a taxi, picked Mac up on his thick stick and took him outside. As they rode uptown to the animal hospital, Mac perched quietly on the back of the front seat next to the professor, and looked out the window. The taxi driver seemed nervous about having such a big bird perched so close by, and he kept looking sideways at him, but Mac paid no attention and remained very still. When they arrived at the animal hospital, the vet examined Mac. He said that he had an upset stomach and should stay there for a couple of days. Two days later the professor telephoned and the vet said that he was well again and could go home.

When the professor came to the animal hospital to get him, Mac was sitting in a cage between two other cages, each of which had a large German shepherd in it. The dogs were barking loudly and Mac was squawking back at them, and he certainly did not seem sick any more. In no time Mac was back home at the university. The following day when the professor came to the office, Fran and Mary said they could tell that Mac had been staying near lots of dogs, because he was "barking" all morning long. Mac then cried out, "Woof, o-o-o-w-w-w, arf arf, r-r-ruff, r-r-ruff," imitating the dogs that he had heard while in the animal hospital!

9. Mac Escapes from a Fire and Nearly Wrecks the Professor's Apartment

One cold winter morning someone shouted "Fire! Fire!" from upstairs, and people began running down from the other offices into the street. The secretaries also said they smelled smoke, and they grabbed their hats and coats and ran outside. It was winter and snowing hard. The professor and Zeki, the other clerk, hurried to grab Mac to take him to safety. The bird had never been out in the cold, so the professor took off his sweater and wrapped it around him, He placed Mac on his stick, and ran outside with him. Smoke was pouring down from upstairs, and in a few minutes the fire engines arrived with their sirens blaring.

Firemen raced into the building with axes and hoses and dashed upstairs. Everyone was worried that the whole building would burn down. In a few minutes the firemen put out the fire, but they did not allow anyone to go back in. There was a lot of smoke damage, and the professor's office was flooded with water from the firemen's hoses.

Since the building had to be closed for a few days, the professor decided to take Mac home with him to his apartment just down the street. He asked one of the firemen to please go inside and bring out Mac's perch, so the bird would have a place to sit in the professor's apartment.

"Sure," said the fireman, "your bird needs a nice place to sit," and in a few minutes he came out carrying the large perch. The professor thanked him and carried Mac, who was partially wrapped in the sweater, to his apartment, while Zeki carried the perch. It was still snowing very hard, and Mac, who had never seen snow before, began licking the snowflakes off his feathers. He kept shaking the snow off his head and his feathers sent up white clouds of snowflakes. He didn't seem to mind the winter weather, because birds' feathers are a natural protection from the cold.

Mac has *broken* a *window*

Once the professor arrived home, he remembered that he had to be away overnight for a business meeting. So he asked a friend to come to the apartment to feed Mac until he returned.

That evening, the professor's friend came to check on Mac and give him water and seeds. When she opened the door, Mac was sitting innocently on his perch. Looking closer, she could not believe what she saw! Once again Mac had unscrewed both his seed and water cups. They had fallen on the floor and made a big puddle. And there were piles of seeds and shells spread all around the room.

"Mac, Mac, what have you done? What an awful mess you have made!" The professor's friend then felt a cold draft coming from the living room window. She went to the window and saw that one of the small windowpanes was lying in pieces on the floor, with empty seed shells all around. She then knew that Mac had been there, and had chewed through the window frame, causing the glass to fall out. "Mac, you bad, bad bird!" she exclaimed. She then went back to Mac's perch to try to attach the cups that he had unscrewed. As she was trying to screw the cups back on, Mac started flapping his wings, opened his beak wide and yelled, **"Get out of here! Get out of here!"** At that, she became so terrified that the hair on her arms and neck stood up, and she later told the professor that she felt that there was something really strange and scary about that bird. "I was too frightened to come any closer. So I telephoned the office and asked Zeki, whom Mac liked very much, to please come over at once to help and to bring more seeds for Mac."

When Zeki arrived, Mac was again sitting calmly on his perch and turned to him with a loud "Hello, Hel-lo!" Zeki put the cups back on and refilled them, and both he and the professor's friend thought it was safe now to leave Mac until the professor returned. "Wait till he sees what an awful mess Mac has made, and what will he say about that broken window? He will surely be very furious with him."

When the professor returned, he was indeed quite furious! "Mac can't stay here any longer!" he exclaimed, "He just can't be trusted. Why, he could wreck my whole apartment!" When it was safe to return, he took Mac back to the office where everyone could keep an eye on him.

For the next few months Mac behaved very well, learning many new words. In fact, the secretaries counted the number of words he could say, which was around 150-- many of them said just at the right moment!

10. Mac Goes to the Zoo

One day an inspector from the city Health Department came to inspect the office, and when he saw Mac, he said that an office was no place for a bird. Everyone protested loudly--- the professor, the secretaries, the clerks, and even people from offices upstairs who often came down to visit Mac. They all loved Mac and felt that they just could not part with him. "Mac works here!" yelled Fran. "We need him," sobbed Mary. "The students and teachers all adore him. . . except for one teacher," exclaimed Phyllis, who by now had begun to like Mac. "It's so much fun having him here!" added Zeki and Peter. The professor pleaded with the inspector, "Please let him stay with us! Please! Please!"

It was no use. The inspector reported to the dean, who was the professor's boss, that Mac would have to find another home. And the dean, who also knew and liked Mac, came to the office to say that he was really terribly sorry, but rules are rules. "A university office is no place for birds, no matter how nice they are. Mac would have to leave!"

But where would he go? This was Mac's home. Who would take such good care of him? It was a very sad time for everyone, especially for the professor. Even Mac seemed to understand. He sat very quietly on his perch, turned his back to the office, and would not eat.

Then the professor had an idea. Perhaps there are macaws in the Central Park Zoo. Mac might find friends there and feel at home again. So he phoned the Zoo and spoke with the birdhouse keeper who said very enthusiastically, "Yes, we would be delighted to have another macaw, especially one that speaks so well. Maybe he could teach the others to speak," and he made an appointment to come to see Mac. When the bird house keeper came to the office Mac said hello to him. He smiled and said Mac was a wonderful bird and would be most welcome at the Zoo. "I'm sure that children from all over the city would love to come to visit Mac and hear him talk."

The professor sadly decided to donate Mac to the Zoo. Everyone was very disappointed and unhappy even though they realized that Mac would have a good home there. The professor loved Mac very dearly as if he were a member of his family. But alas, there was nothing he could do but get Mac ready for the trip to the Zoo.

A few days later, the Zoo sent a large station wagon to pick up Mac. The people in the office all got together to pack his perch, a few of his toys, his food, and his cage, and they gathered outside to say goodbye. The professor carried Mac on his big stick to the car, and rode with him to the Zoo.

It was a bright, sunny afternoon when they arrived. To the professor's surprise they were met by a large crowd of people. There were newspaper reporters, photographers and television cameramen. "Whom are they waiting for?" asked the professor. "Why, for Mac, of course," said the director of the zoo who greeted them. "He's a big celebrity now. Everybody has heard about this wonderful talking bird and the professor who is donating him to the Zoo."

The professor got out of the car with Mac, still perched on his stick, and everyone came close to look. The reporters crowded around and asked lots of questions and took many photos. Mac became a bit frightened by the commotion and moved back on the stick closer to the

Mac escapes

professor. The professor then asked the people not to come too close, as Mac was not used to so much noise and crowding, and if he became scared he could bite very hard.

11. Mac Escapes

Just then the City Park Commissioner arrived to welcome Mac and to have his picture taken with him. He reached out suddenly to pat Mac on the head, but by doing that he startled Mac, who then leaped off the perch and flew high into the air. Mac circled upward above the crowd with his beautiful bright red wings outstretched. Higher and higher he flew until he landed on the topmost branch of a nearby very tall tree. It was the first time he had ever flown outside. Nobody had ever expected that he would fly off like that.

The professor became very upset, and with all the reporters watching and taking pictures, he cried out to Mac to come down. But Mac paid no attention. He just sat there looking down from his high perch, squawking, "Caw! Caw! Caw!"

"Hey, Mac," shouted the professor. "Come down, Mac!" Then all the people joined in, shouting "Mac, Mac, Mac . . .Come down, Mac!" But Mac didn't budge.

The Park Commissioner decided to call the Fire Department to see if they could reach Mac with one of their tall ladders. In a few minutes two large fire engines arrived. The firemen raised their longest ladder against the tree, but it was too tall, and Mac was sitting on the highest branch, far out of reach.

Everyone continued calling to Mac, and the professor held up a big red apple, one of Mac's favorite fruits. "Hey, Mac, want an apple?" he shouted. But Mac did not seem to be interested. The firemen, seeing that they could not reach him, folded their ladder and returned to their firehouse. Then Mac let out another loud squawk and took off again, flying high into the sky, disappearing beyond the treetops in the park. The whole scene of Mac's unexpected escape was captured by the TV cameramen and broadcast live by the radio announcers, and on the next day reported in the newspapers.

In the meantime the professor was terribly worried. What would happen to Mac? How could Mac take care of himself? Was Mac gone forever? Would he ever see him again? People then scattered in every direction to look for him, but he was nowhere to be seen. The professor continued searching until evening when it became too dark to search any further. Sadly, with tears in his eyes, he went home.

That night the professor could not sleep. He worried about Mac who was probably perched somewhere on a strange tree, all alone in the park's dark forest.

Very early the next morning the professor got up and took a tape recorder with him to the park. He had made recordings of Mac talking some time before he donated him, so he thought he would play Mac's voice as loud as he could, and perhaps Mac would recognize it and come down. He walked for hours through the park, playing Mac's voice over and over and calling out to him. But there was no answer. As he wandered uphill and down among the tall trees, he asked if anyone had seen a big red bird, but nobody had.

12. Mac is Found!

By late afternoon, the professor was feeling more and more unhappy. He felt sure that his friend was gone forever. Just then a little boy came running up to him and asked, "Are you the man looking for a big red bird?" "Yes, I sure am. Have you seen him?" asked the professor nervously.

"He's just over that hill, high up in a tree. C'mon, I'll show you." They ran up the hill and down the other side to the tree. A crowd had gathered in the meantime, and looking way up, the professor spotted Mac perched on the highest branch of a tall sycamore tree.

"Hello, Mac! Hi Mac!" shouted the professor several times. To the professor's joy Mac looked down and answered him with a loud squawk. "Come on, Mac" he repeated, "Come on down, Mac!" But Mac seemed in no mood to fly down.

Some park employees came with a ladder, but it, too, turned out to be much too short. They decided to call the Fire Department again, and in a few minutes a fire engine arrived--the same one as the day before.

"We'll never get your bird," said one of the firemen, "he's up too high, and our ladders probably cannot reach him. We'll try again to get Mac for you, but I don't think we can." The firemen climbed the ladder once more to try to reach Mac's branch, but again the ladder was just not long enough. After a while, the firemen gave up, waved goodbye to Mac, wished the professor better luck, and drove their fire engine back to the firehouse.

In the meantime, word had spread that Mac was seen again, and more and more people gathered. Another television crew arrived, hoping to show Mac being captured, but Mac was stubborn and would not come down, even though the professor knew that by now he must be very hungry.

At that moment two men from the Central Park Zoo arrived bringing a red macaw from the zoo's bird house. They said his name was Captain Hook, and maybe if Mac saw him, he might come down. When Captain Hook saw Mac, he starting calling up to him. Mac leaned forward on the branch and called back, "Caw . . . Caw . . .Caw!" For a long time they just kept squawking back and forth to each other, but Mac would not budge.

The park employees had prepared a net and a cage for Mac, but he did not respond. After about an hour, they began to think that it was hopeless to catch Mac. Even Captain Hook gave up and stopped calling up to him. The TV crew, however, refused to give up. "Maybe Mac will change his mind. He would be great news to put on television tonight."

Luis tempts Mac with an apple

Just then a young man who had been watching from the crowd came up to the professor and whispered, "I can get Mac for you!"

"What do you mean, you can get him for me?" asked the professor, very surprised. "That's a very tall tree. I don't think anyone can climb it."

"I am used to climbing tall trees," said the young man. "In my country I used to climb very high palm trees all the time to pick the coconuts."

"Do you really think you can catch Mac? What is your name?"

"My name is Luis Gomez, and I come from the Dominican Republic, and maybe that's where Mac came from too. I will talk to him in Spanish and maybe he will understand. Let me try to get him."

The men from the Zoo didn't want him to climb the tree. They were afraid that he might fall and be injured or even killed. But Luis insisted, and finally they agreed to let him climb up, saying "O.K., but be very careful!" and they gave him a net to catch Mac.

The professor, who had brought a supply of apples for Mac, gave two to Luis, who put them in his pocket. He took off his shoes, grabbed the net, and began climbing the tall tree. Slowly he went up the trunk, moving from branch to branch, higher and higher, until he reached the branch near the top that Mac was perched on.

Mac had been watching him all the time, and when Luis moved slowly toward him on the branch, he looked at Luis very suspiciously. He then began moving farther and farther out. Luis then took out an apple and held it out to Mac. He began speaking softly to him in Spanish, encouraging him to come closer. At first Mac paid no attention, then he cocked his head and seemed to be listening. Luis continued talking to him, holding out the nice juicy apple to tempt him. Mac was now very hungry, and he began to move just a little closer to the apple. Luis could not go out any further because the branch was beginning to sag, and he was afraid that he might topple out of the tree.

Mac could not take his eyes off that bright red apple. After a few minutes he began to approach Luis. Nearer and nearer he came, staring hungrily at that delicious apple, while Luis kept talking sweetly to him. At last, Mac could resist the apple no longer, and he reached out with his beak to grab it. The professor and everyone on the ground quietly held their breath.

At that moment Luis suddenly threw the net over Mac and grabbed him, pressing his wings against his body to prevent his escape. Holding Mac gently under his left arm wrapped in the net, Luis slowly worked his way down. Mac screamed angrily, louder than he ever had. He was frightened and furious! But his screams didn't help, and when they reached the ground, the men from the Zoo had the cage ready. They leaped forward, grabbed Mac, and quickly plopped him into the cage.

Mac was safe at last! A loud cheer burst forth from the crowd that had gathered, from the zoo employees, and even from the television crew who had caught the whole scene of Mac's capture on film, and would show it that night on the evening news. Mac, however, kept on squawking loudly. He was not happy about being yanked out of the tree and losing his freedom. He was also very hungry and thirsty.

13. Mac Has a New Home

The professor walked with the men from the Zoo to the bird house where Mac was placed in a huge cage alongside his new friend, Captain Hook. There were many other birds in nearby cages--parrots, toucans, and other types of macaws. The professor was glad that Mac was now safe. He turned and said goodbye to Mac! and promised to visit him soon. Mac was still too shaken up to answer, but he did look at the professor and tried to move as close to him as he could in the cage.

That evening the television news programs were filled with the story of Mac's escape and recapture, and the following day his picture appeared in newspapers around the country.

Mac in his new home at the zoo

Captain Hook   Mac

A few days later the professor came to visit Mac in his new home. He brought him an apple and some peanuts. When Mac saw him he began bouncing up and down and cried out "HEL-LO, HEL-LO! He was so happy to see the professor again and seemed to like his new home. Although the professor was sorry that Mac could not stay with him any longer, he was glad that Mac was now in a very nice place and would not be alone, and he would have many new friends among the birds. He promised to visit Mac as often as he could.

A week later the professor came again to visit Mac. He was now in a new cage with several other macaws. There was a big crowd gathered around the cage, and as the professor came closer, he saw Mac right in front, sitting on a perch. There were many children watching and laughing. Mac was talking very loudly, saying "Hello, Mac! Gimme a kiss! One--two--three--four--five--six, pick up sticks! Apple, banana, orange, strawberry, carrot . ." and many more words.

The professor had brought another handful of peanuts for Mac, and when Mac saw him, he moved close to the bars of the cage, and said "HEL-LO, HEL-LO." The professor put his hand near the cage and Mac reached out, stuck his head through the bars, opened his beak wide and gently grabbed a peanut. He then said, "Is that good?" The children roared with laughter and shouted, "Hey, was that good, Mac?" Then Mac surprised them even more and said, "M-m-m that's good!"

The children were delighted with Mac and kept talking to him. And, of course, Mac loved all that attention, and he repeating the words he knew. The professor was very glad that Mac did not say "Get out of here!" However he did yell "HELP! HELP ME!" a couple of times, and the children wondered whether he really needed help, but the professor explained that Mac just enjoyed saying it.

The professor continued to make frequent visits to the Zoo. Every time Mac saw him, he would fly over to the front of the large cage, hang on the bars, and say "HEL-LO, HE-LO!" Even

Mac's friend, Captain Hook, began to imitate what Mac was saying, and the professor was quite amused one day to hear both of them speaking to each other. Captain Hook would say "Hello, Mac," and Mac answered with his usual "HEL-LO!"

The birdhouse keepers said they enjoyed taking care of Mac, and they taught him many new things to say. "You know, professor," said one of the keepers, "I have been counting how many words Mac knows, and we now are sure that he can say at least two hundred! He is surely the smartest macaw we've ever met! Macaws live very long, so if we're lucky, we'll have him here with us for many years."

And if YOU ever visit the Central Park Zoo, go to the birdhouse and look for Mac. Bring along a few peanuts, and maybe he'll say "HEL-LO", "M-m-m-that's good!" or more of his favorite expressions. . . and perhaps he'll even tell you "Gimme a kiss!"

A note to my readers

You may remember that when the professor brought Mac to Central Park to donate him to the Zoo, there were many newspaper, radio, and TV reporters present who had been invited to meet "the big talking bird" and report the event. No one expected that Mac would suddenly leap off the professor's arm and fly away, but when he did, the reporters realized that they had an even more newsworthy story on their hands. So they remained in the park for two days until Mac was finally recaptured, put into a cage, and brought to the park's birdhouse.

On the following pages are some of those articles and photos that appeared in many newspapers throughout the country and even in Europe. Immediately afterward is a page of photographs of Mac that were taken in the professor's office at New York University.

Please also read the back cover to learn a little about the author (the professor) and the famous Native American artist who drew those pretty pictures of Mac.

DAILY NEWS

NEW YORK'S PICTURE NEWSPAPER ®

New York, N.Y. 10017, Saturday, July 28,

INTERNATIONAL

Herald Tribune

Published with The New York Times and The Washington Post

PARIS, SATURDAY-SUNDAY, JULY 28-29,

* *

The New York Times

The Record

Friend of the People It Serves

MONDAY, JULY 30, 1973

Serving New Jersey and New York
From Hackensack, N. J. 07602

The Topeka State Journal

Topeka, Kansas, Saturday Evening, July 28.

10¢

rice for carrier delivery

Official city newspaper · Official county newspaper

Talking Bird Takes a Flier

A Macaw on a Lark Is No Dodo

By PETER COUTROS

For a red-necked macaw, Big Mac's no dodo. He has 100 words in his vocabulary. A few more and he could be a politician. Big Mac can also fly, not having forgotten his heritage, as some people thought.

Actually, the only thing you can fault Big Mac for is that he doesn't listen. Gerard Wolfe could tell you about that, if Gerard Wolfe doesn't have laryngitis by now.

Wolfe is a New York University language professor and up until 2:30 yesterday Big Mac was the professor's pride and joy, both brilliant and articulate. Sadly for Big Mac, the girls who work in Prof. Wolfe's office preferred his calls to the macaw's verbosity.

The Girls Got Rid of Him

The stenos didn't mind Big Mac's cries for "apples" and "Bananas" or "peanuts," but those screams of "He-e-eelp!" were more than they could stand, so when one of them read in the paper that two of Central Park's macaws had been stolen and only one returned, they suggested—none too subtly—that the good professor take his bird to the park and make a big-name donor of himself.

And that is just what was happening at

2:30 p.m. outside John Fitzgerald's office. Fitzgerald is the zoo's director.

Media representatives were there to suitably record the event and some guy from one of the networks—a sort of bleached Howard Cosell—put the bird down when Big Mac didn't talk. What Mac was waiting for was some dough. Or maybe an apple or banana.

The Macaw Flies Away

That's when Big Mac lit out. He flew 100 feet east and 40 feet up and came to rest on a limb of an oak, leaving the professor, park personnel and various reporters up a tree.

At first, everybody chuckled; some lark. One by one, they called to Mac. They whistled. They made funny jokes. Big Mac responded not at all, least of all to the bad jokes.

Wolfe implored the bird, he beseeched him.

He played to his sympathy and his liking for bananas, apples and peanuts. He used Big Mac's own taped "Help!" All for nothing.

Then Fitzgerald climbed a tree and sawed the limb. That's when Big Mac took off, turning first toward Fifth Ave. Seeing the traffic there, he veered into the park, got lost in the trees and right now he must be the prettiest damn bird ever seen flying around Central Park.

NEWS photo by Jim Garrett

Dr. Gerard Wolfe of NYU with his macaw, Mac, at the zoo.

Bye, bye birdy

Prof. Gerard Wolfe of New York University, in top photo, shows off Mac, his pet macaw, before donating the bird to New York's Central Park Zoo Thursday. Later, Prof. Wolfe uses a megaphone, bottom, in an attempt to retrieve the bird after Mac took off for parts unknown. By the day's end, Mac was still at large.

ON THE LAM — Bowing to demands from secretaries in his office, New York University language Professor Gerald Wolfe agreed to present his prized red-necked macaw to the Central Park Zoo. It seems that while the ladies could put up with Big Mac blabbing its 100-word vocabulary, they couldn't stomach its shreiks of "Heeelllpp." Just before the bird was to be turned over, however, it flew the coop. When last seen yesterday by assembled media men and zoologists, it had sprinted toward Fifth Avenue, and then peeled off into the wilds of the park.

* * *

Central Park, it appears, is not for the birds.

Mac the Macaw took off for parts unknown Thursday during ceremonies at which his owner, Prof. Gerard Wolfe of New York University, was giving him to the zoo to replace Poppi, another macaw stolen last weekend.

"I've always had that effect on pretty birds," said New York parks administrator **Richard Clurman.** Mac was sitting on Wolfe's shoulder when he took off for a perch in a tree-top. Emergency measures were put in force. The professor played a tape-recording of Mac's own voice. Captain Hook, another macaw, was brought over to try to coax the bird down. Nothing worked.

Mac, his red body, blue and green wings and black and white head flashing in the sun, flew off—this time to a high oak. "When he gets hungry he'll come down," said Wolfe. But Mac, who speaks pretty good English, took off for the West. His last words were "help," "apple," "banana."

Metropolitan Briefs

If a Macaw Asks Way Back to Zoo . . .

The city's Parks Department learned that a bird in the hand is worth two in a tree, when a pet macaw flew away as its owner was donating it to the Central Park Zoo. Richard M. Clurman, the Parks Administrator, was thanking Gerard Wolfe, a language professor at New York University, for his gift when Mac, the professor's vocal macaw, flew into a nearby tree and refused to come down even as tape recordings of its voice were played to entice it. After an hour in the tree, the bird, a brightly colored species of parrot with a vocabulary of 100 words, flew away and has not been seen since. "I've always had that effect on pretty birds," Mr. Clurman said ruefully.

Macaw, Lured by Apple, Recaptured

By ROBERT D. McFADDEN

A motley macaw named Mac—who took the occasion of his own presentation to the Central Park Zoo Thursday to fly away—was captured in the upper reaches of a lofty Central Park sycamore yesterday afternoon by an agile Dominican youth with a tempter's apple and a spiel of soothing, cooing Spanish.

The blue, red and orange bird "squawked like mad" when 21-year-old Luis Gomez grabbed him by the tail on a slender branch 70 feet up in the tree behind the bandshell near the 72d Street Drive.

But Mr. Gomez pinned Mac's wings back and hung on, ending a short saga of stubborn independence that began Thursday when he flew off his owner's shoulder as he was being donated as a replacement for another macaw stolen last weekend. After disappearing in the treetops, he was not seen till 12:30 P.M. yesterday.

Thereafter, it was a frustrating afternoon for those on the ground.

'Squawk' Fails

In an effort to lure Mac down from his perch, a New York University language professor who had donated the creature to the zoo stood at the tree's base and shouted, "Squawk! Squawk!" Prof. Gerard Wolfe also played tape recordings of Mac's own voice.

But Mac was unimpressed. Parks Department employes brought out bananas and bird seed. Still, Mac was unimpressed.

He didn't even pay much attention when John Fitzgerald, director of the zoo,

brought out Pinito—one of the two macaws stolen last weekend who was later found in Westchester County —to talk to Mac. At least that was the intent.

"They both called a little," said Theodore Mastroianni, deputy parks commissioner, "but I don't know whether they were actually talking to each other."

Parks Department climbers and pruners, as they are called, brought out their "cherry-picker"—a hydraulic-lift platform for lofty work—but it reached up only 40 feet, well below the level of Mac's perch.

And it began to look like a hopeless cause when the climbers and pruners declined to climb for the macaw, saying it was not in their contract.

Then, according to Mr. Mastroianni, along came Mr. Gomez, who said he had learned how to climb trees in the Dominican Republic before moving here four years ago, and "pleaded with us three or four times" to be allowed to go after the macaw.

'Talking Very Quietly'

After first declining the offer, Mr. Mastroianni finally gave his approval, but emphasized caution.

Mr. Gomez took off his shirt and his blue suede, knee-high boots, stuffed an apple in his pocket and swung himself up into the branches of the huge sycamore, which has a girth at the base of nearly 11 feet.

"He went from branch to branch to branch; it was just marvelous," said Mr. Mastroianni, who added that Mr.

Gomez reached the upper fringes of the tree, where the bird was, in "15 seconds."

"The bird was not on a heavy branch," the deputy commissioner said, "so Mr. Gomez broke a twig off, put the apple on the end of it and had to lean quite far to even get it near the bird.

"He was leaning over and talking to the bird very quietly and smoothly in Spanish. At first, the bird had his back turned, but then he started to respond. He looked around at Mr. Gomez and slowly began walking along the branch toward him.

"It was like a little ballet on the branch. It was very beautiful."

Mr. Mastroianni said that, when Mac drew near enough, he began taking "a couple of pecks" at the apple, which Mr. Gomez gradually drew back toward himself. Then, the young man "snatched the bird by the tail," and the bird "squawked like mad and was jumping all over," trying to break free, Mr. Mastroianni said.

But Mr. Gomez pinned his wings back, avoiding the bird's dangerous beak and claws, and descended slowly, climbing down with one hand while holding the bird in the other. Near the bottom, at about 2 P.M., Mr. Fitzgerald whisked a net over Mac and took him back to the zoo, where he is to become a companion of Pinito.

"It was amazing, incredible," said Mr. Mastroianni, who added that Parks Administrator Richard M. Clurman had invited Mr. Gomez to his office next Monday to receive a "certificate of ap-

preciation and, if he wants one, a job with the Parks Department.

As for Mac, who acquired a vocabulary of about 100 words as Professor Wolfe's pet over the last three years, freedom and flying days appear to be over. Mr. Mastroianni said the zoo planned to clip his wings "so he won't fly away,"

Mac, a somewhat mischievous—and definitely loquacious macaw, in captivity at the Central Park Zoo.

Bilingual Macaw Is Caged

Piece of Apple Proves Too Tempting

By ARTHUR MULLIGAN

Big Mac, the real macaw, not only has an English vocabulary of 100 words or more; he also has a nice understanding of Spanish. probably a throwback to his Latin American heritage.

Big Mac, who flew away over Central Park treetops Thursday evening, got his feet back on the ground yesterday when a 21-year-old youth from the Dominican Republic scrambled 70 feet up a Central Park sycamore tree and using dulcet Spanish phrases talked him down.

The brightly plumaged macaw, the property of Gerard Wolfe, a New York University language professor, had his 15 - minute Spanish lesson in a 90-foot tree overlooking the bandshell on the Central Park Mall at 72d St.

No band was playing at that hour, 2 p.m., but the soft murmurings of Luis Gomez, who came here from the Dominican Republic four years ago, must have been music to the big bird's ears.

Frightened at all the attention being paid him by a television crew, Park Commissioner Richard M. Clurman, Deputy Commissioner Theodore Mastroianni, zoo director John Fitzgerald and assorted bystanders, Big Mac seemed loath to leave his lofty perch. Even his master, Wolfe, could not persuade him to come down.

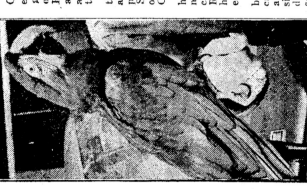

Big Mac—those dulcet Spanish phrases got 'im.

Then Gomez, who lives at 362 W. 52d St., prevailed upon the park officials to let him climb the tree.

"He took off his sports shirt and shoes and was up that tree in 15 or 20 seconds," Mastroianni said. "I couldn't believe how fast he climbed."

Gomez stuck a piece of apple on the end of a loose branch, and extended it toward Big Mac, talking all the time in low tones. Big Mac, who at first appeared indifferent and kept his back to Gomez, finally turned toward him and came close enough for Gomez to grab him.

Then, Gomez climbed down and turned Big Mac over to Fitzgerald.

Wolfe had brought the bird to the zoo Thursday to replace a macaw that had been stolen. But Big Mac got flustered and flew off.

Wolfe, who is director of foreign languages at NYU's Continuing Education School, said he would try to arrange a scholarship for Gomez to study English and take other courses there. Gomez is the building superintendent of the apartment house in which he lives.

The professor says goodbye to his friend Mac in Central Park.

Here are a few photos of Mac taken in the professor's office.

Mac inside his new cage

Mac was sitting on top of the cabinet door just before he climbed inside and pulled both doors shut. He then began to sing loudly.

Mac meets *Matchka* the cat on the professor's desk.